LILLY AND MINOT

Visit the New Orleans Oil Spill

WRITTEN BY WILLIAM SARGENT
ILLUSTRATED BY JULIA PURINTON

Copyright © 2010 Bill Sargent
All rights reserved.
ISBN: 1453772138
ISBN-13: 9781453772133

Lilly and Minot
How It All Began

Lilly and Minot live at a dairy farm in the little town of Ipswich, north of Boston. They became famous when Lilly taught kids how to ride her bull-friend, Minot.

Their unbounded curiosity and desire to help others have led to great adventures around the world, from leading the Mardi Gras parade in New Orleans to learning about Minot's Indian bovine counterparts.

In this book, the famous pair travel to New Orleans to help clean up the oil spill in the Gulf of Mexico.

Dedicated to the Gulf of Mexico.
Lilly thinks it has some wonderful people.
Minot thinks it has some wonderful fish.

It was a warm sultry day when Lilly and Minot crossed over the river into New Orleans. Stately oak trees swayed beside the Mississippi, and broad-leaved magnolias flowered in the evening air.

A short man with glasses and curly hair met them at the University gate.

"Bienvenue. I'm Dr. Oliver Ivor van Heerenden Houck. You must be Lilly and Minot."

"It's so nice to be back in New Orleans," said Lilly.

"I wish it were for a happier occasion," said Ivor. "The oil spill here in the Gulf of Mexico has created a terrible mess."

"We want to help clean up the birds and turtles that have been covered in oil. The poor things," said Lilly.

"That would be wonderful. I'll pick you up at your campground tomorrow and drop you off at one of the cleaning stations. But right now, the faculty wants to see me about something. I'll see you tomorrow morning at 5:30 sharp!"

The next morning Lilly and Minot woke up to the "thwock, thwock, thwock" of a huge orange-and-white Coast Guard helicopter hovering over their trailer. A man in a diving suit dropped down on a cable to help them get into a large cage so they could be lifted aboard.

"Bienvenue. I'm commander Mary, Russell, Desiree, Honore, Valeree, Thad Allen. I think you already know Dr. Houck."

"I didn't know you meant you would pick us up in a HELICOPTER!" exclaimed Lilly. "But I'm so honored to meet you, commander Allen. You guys did such a wonderful job rescuing people off their roofs during Hurricane Katrina."

"All in a day's work," said Commander Allen. "And you must be Lilly and that famous bull, Minot. Weren't you the Fatted Calf in our Mardi Gras Parade last year?"

"He's a still a little sensitive about being called fat," whispered Lilly.

"Or a calf!" said Minot, loud enough for everyone to hear.

"Oh my gosh, look at the size of that spill," said Lilly.

A large patch of rust-colored oil stretched as far as the eye could see.

"The spill is already larger than the state of Delaware. We're afraid that we might never be able to stop the oil from pouring out, and then we could have sixty million gallons of oil a day gushing up out of that well."

"That would make it the biggest oil spill in history!" said Lilly.

"Yup. Unfortunately, it would. See those ships over there? They are operating ten small robot submarines that are trying to cut off the flow of oil from a burst pipe a mile below the surface. They have to turn off some valves, but they haven't had any luck so far."

"That big ship on our left is trying to lower that huge box over the burst pipe so they can collect the oil and pump it to the surface. It's kind of like trying to use a hat to stop water gushing out of a fire hose."

"A Cajun chapeau!" said Minot triumphantly.

"No, a Cajun cap!" corrected Lilly.

"Whatever it is, it's bigger than our barn," said Minot.

"Yes, it's almost five stories high and weighs a hundred tons," said commander Allen. "They have to lower it a mile down and steady it with submarines so they can cover the broken pipe."

"Sounds pretty difficult," said Lilly.

"Yup. It's never been done in water this deep before. It's so cold down there that ice can block the container so you can't pump the oil to the surface."

"That oil rig over there to our right is trying to drill another relief well deep down into the earth below the ocean so they can find the pipe and fill it with concrete to stop the spill."

"That sounds very difficult!"

"Yes. The pipe is only seven inches across. They have to find it a mile below the surface and several thousand feet underground!"

"That sounds almost impossible!"

"We hope not. Otherwise this spill could go on for years."

"That looks like a dead bird floating on the water."

"Probably a pelican or gannet," said Dr. Houck. "When birds see an oil spill they think it is an oil slick made by big fish feeding on small, oily fish, so they dive into the spill and get covered with oil. Then they can't fly, so eventually they drown or starve to death."

"That's just awful," said Lilly.

"Is that a turtle?" asked Minot.

"Yup. They are having a terrible time out here. But it's the things you can't see that could be doing the most damage. See those planes over there? They are spraying chemicals called dispersants on the oil. They make the oil sink."

"That should be good for the birds," Said Lilly.

"Yes, but it's bad for the fish. Spring is the worst time of year for an oil spill. All the fish have just laid their eggs and now they have either hatched or are still drifting in the water. The little fish can be killed by both the oil and the chemicals. Right now we have a lot of eggs from bluefin tuna in the water. We are very worried about them. There is even a pod of sperm whales, which could get sick and drown in the oil. It could take years for this ocean to fully recover."

"The poor animals," said Minot.

"The poor fishermen!" said Lilly.

"Over there is the Breton Wildlife Refuge," said Dr. Houck. "It was started by President Theodore Roosevelt to protect the terns, plovers and pelicans that nest on the Chandeleur Islands."

"They are so beautiful! It's so sad to see them all covered with oil."

The helicopter lowered Lilly and Minot onto a cleaning station and they took their places between a fisherman from Terrebonne and a woman from Des Moines.

"Hi, my name is Throung Nygeyan, but you can call me Tong."

"Where do you come from, Mr. Tong?"

"I came from Vietnam. I escaped on a small boat. We were adrift for eleven days without food or water. Everybody was praying to Buddha and Jesus. I was so scared and so seasick! But we were finally rescued and I was able to bring my family to the United States and my uncle asked me to help him on his shrimp boat. A few years ago, I was able to buy my own boat so I was finally my own captain."

"That's an incredible story," said Lilly. "What was it like fishing for shrimp?"

"You can't believe how beautiful it was, fishing at night. There were so many stars, and you could hear the dolphins and turtles coming up for air. It made me feel as small as a shrimp!"

"Wow!"

"The boats would all cluster together between the islands waiting for the tide to turn. It looked like a city of lights. As soon as the tide turned the shrimp would start coming in and everyone would jostle for position. Sometimes, we would spray water at the other boats. Everyone would be laughing and yelling and hauling in millions of shrimp."

"It made me feel very proud to be able to go out every night and bring back seafood for the people of the United States, who helped me so much! Now I feel useless, so I help clean these poor birds and turtles. They are like me, you know, innocent victims of this terrible oil spill."

"You're a poet, Mr. Tong."

"No. I'm just a fisherman who wants to help," said Mr. Tong, sadly.

"You are doing good work," said Lilly.

"Sometimes, I wonder if we're doing more harm than good. Perhaps we should have let Mother Nature clean up herself."

"You are a wise man, Mr. Tong."

"No. I don't have any wisdom, but I do have this pearl I found in my uncle's oyster beds last year. I would like to give it to both of you."

"Oh, a pearl of great worth," said Minot, sagely.

"We will put it on a shelf in the barn to remind us of what happened to the Gulf of Mexico," said Lilly.

Made in the USA
Charleston, SC
12 June 2011